USBORNE FIRST READING
Level Three

The Castle That Jack Built

Lesley Sims
Illustrated by Mike Gordon

Danny the Dragon

Russell Punter
Illustrated by Peter Cottrill

The Boy Who cried Wolf

Retold by Mairi Mackinnon
Illustrated by Mike and Carl Gordon

Chicken Licken

retold by Russell Punter
Illustrated by Ann Kronheimer

Tom Thumb

Retold by Katie Daynes
Illustrated by Wesley Robins

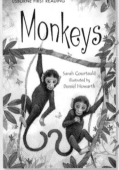

Monkeys

Sarah Courtauld
Illustrated by Daniel Howarth

Dinosaurs

Conrad Mason
Illustrated by Daniel Howarth

The Magic Pear Tree

Retold by Rosie Dickins

The Magic Porridge Pot

A story by The Brothers Grimm
Retold by Mike and Carl Gordon

The Lion and the Mouse

Retold by Susanna Davidson

Illustrated by John Joven

Reading consultant: Alison Kelly

The sun beat down on
the dry ground.

"It's much too hot for me," said Chief Mouse. "Let's go back home to our burrow."

"I think I'll stay here," said Little Mouse, "and eat some more seeds."

"You can't stay on your own," said Chief Mouse. "You're too little."

You're too little to do *anything* on your own.

"Follow me everyone,"
said Chief Mouse.

He led them through
clumps of grass...

He led them across
shallow streams...

...and under shady trees.

Poor Little
Mouse couldn't
keep up.

Now he was all alone.

He was also... LOST!

Ahead, Little Mouse saw a large hill. "I'll climb the hill," he thought.

Then I might be able to see the others.

Little Mouse began
to climb.

"This is a very strange hill," thought Little Mouse.

"It keeps moving up and down."

"I'm beginning to
think it's not a hill
at all..."

Then Little Mouse
turned around.

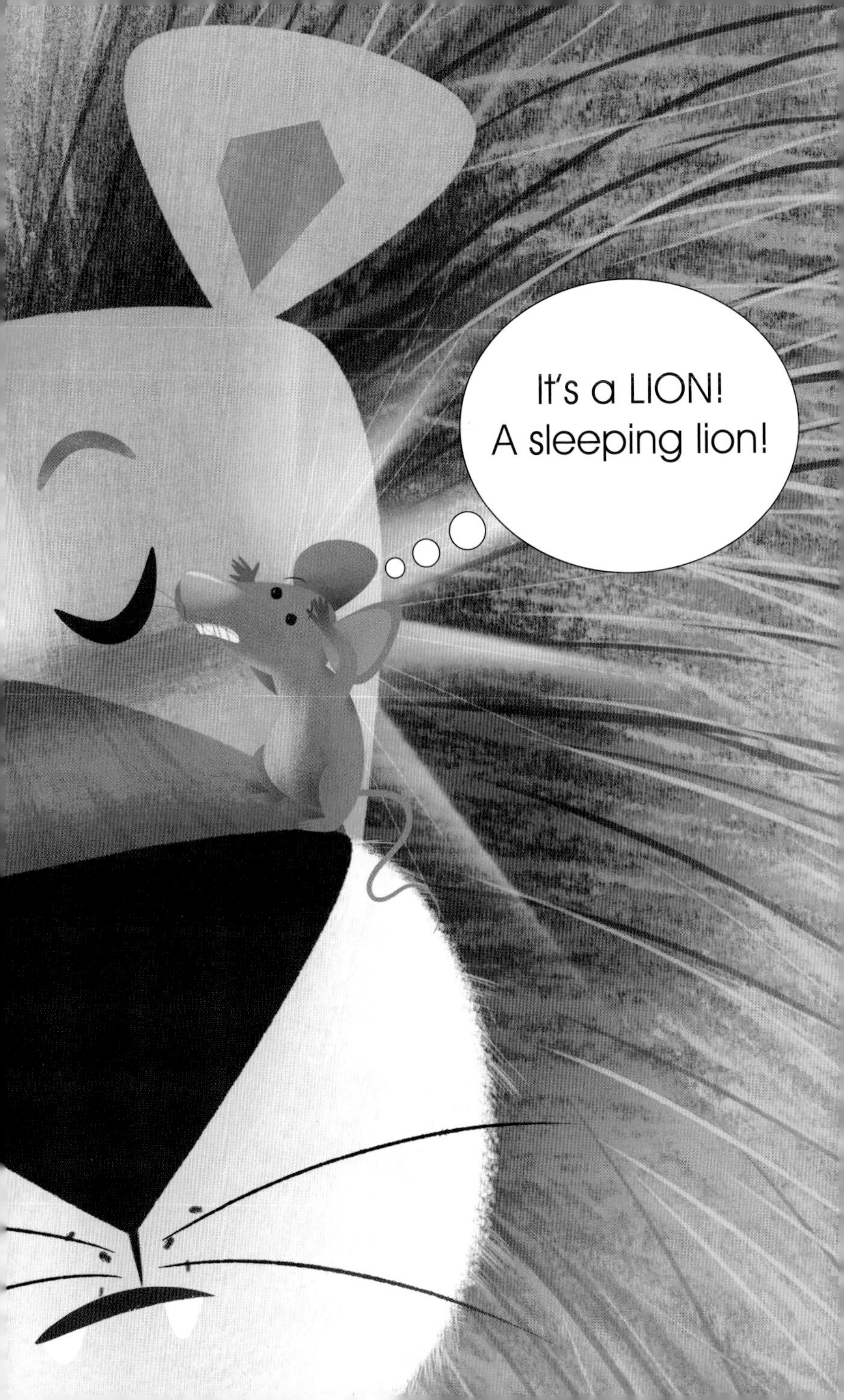
It's a LION!
A sleeping lion!

Little Mouse squeaked so loudly, Lion woke up.

Lion did *not* look happy.

Little Mouse tried to run...

...but Lion caught
   him by the tail.

"You woke me up," said
Lion. "And now I'm going
to EAT YOU!"

21

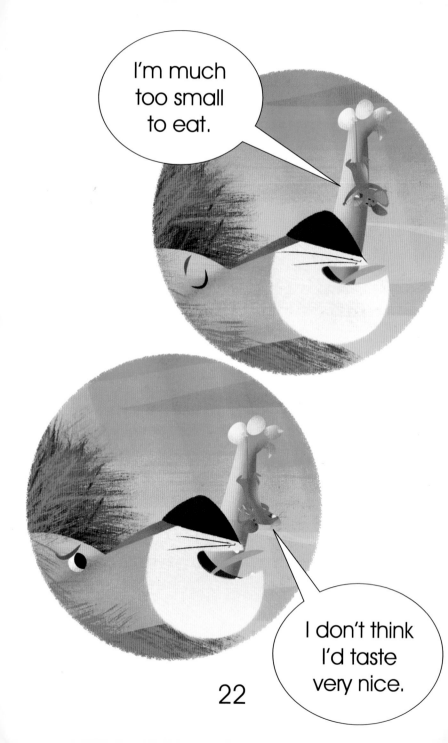

22

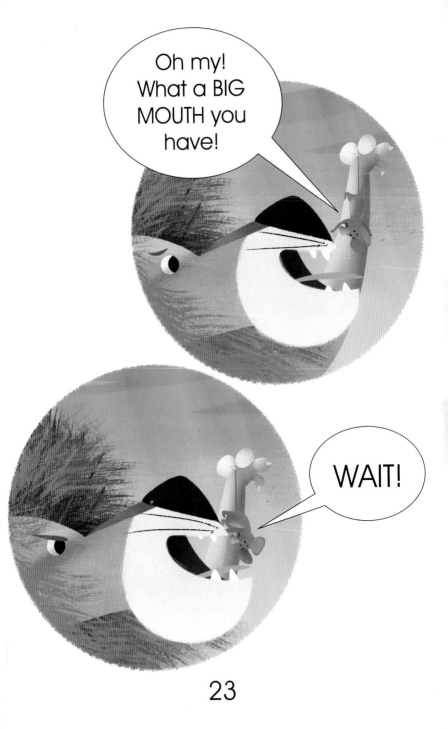

23

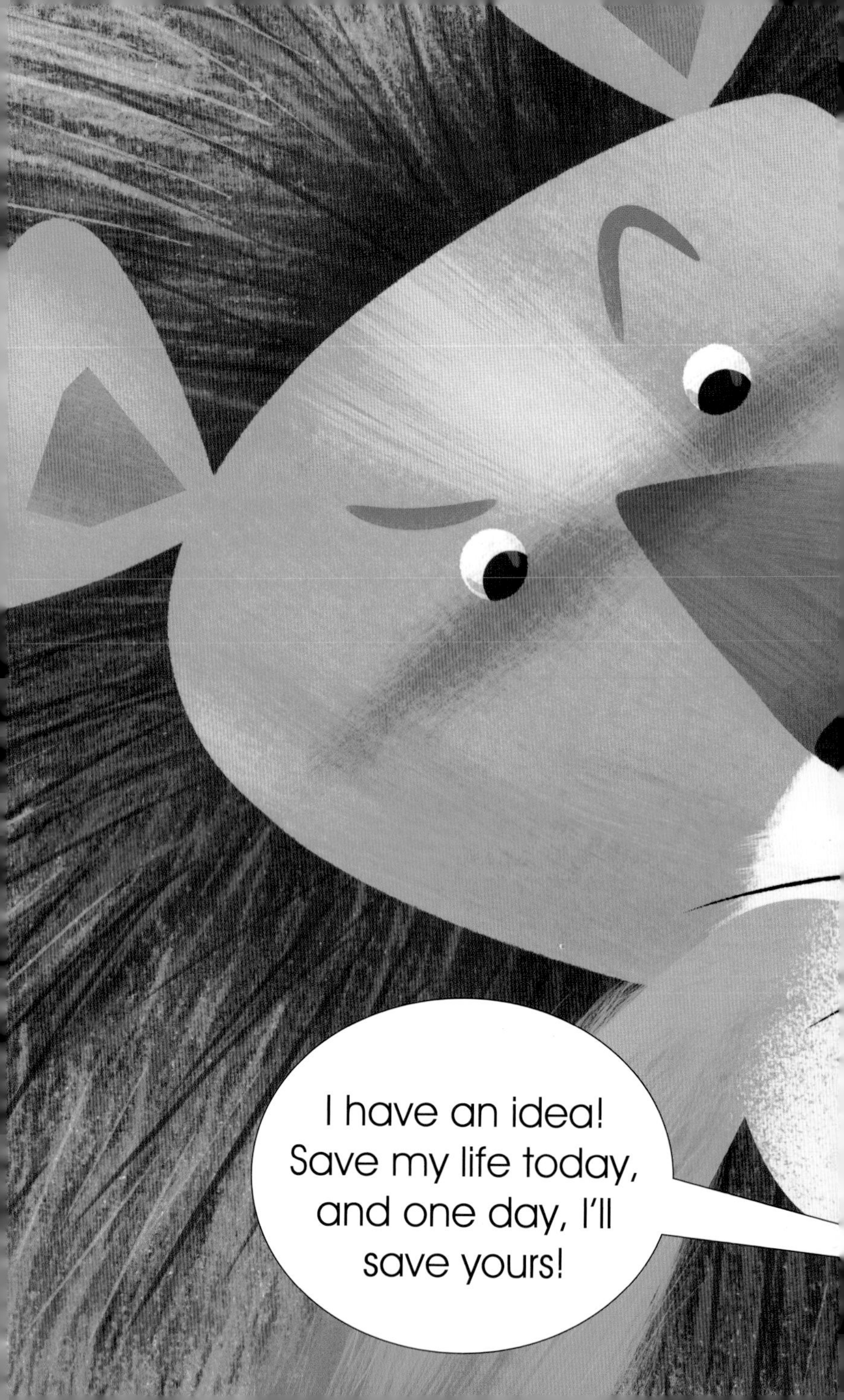
I have an idea! Save my life today, and one day, I'll save yours!

How Lion laughed!

Ha! Ha! Ha!

"As if YOU could ever save
ME," he chuckled.

Haaaaaaa!

"But you've made
me laugh, little friend, so
I'll let you go."

27

Then Little Mouse turned around... and fled.

Whew! That was close!

Little Mouse finally found his burrow. He told the other mice his story.

They all laughed too.

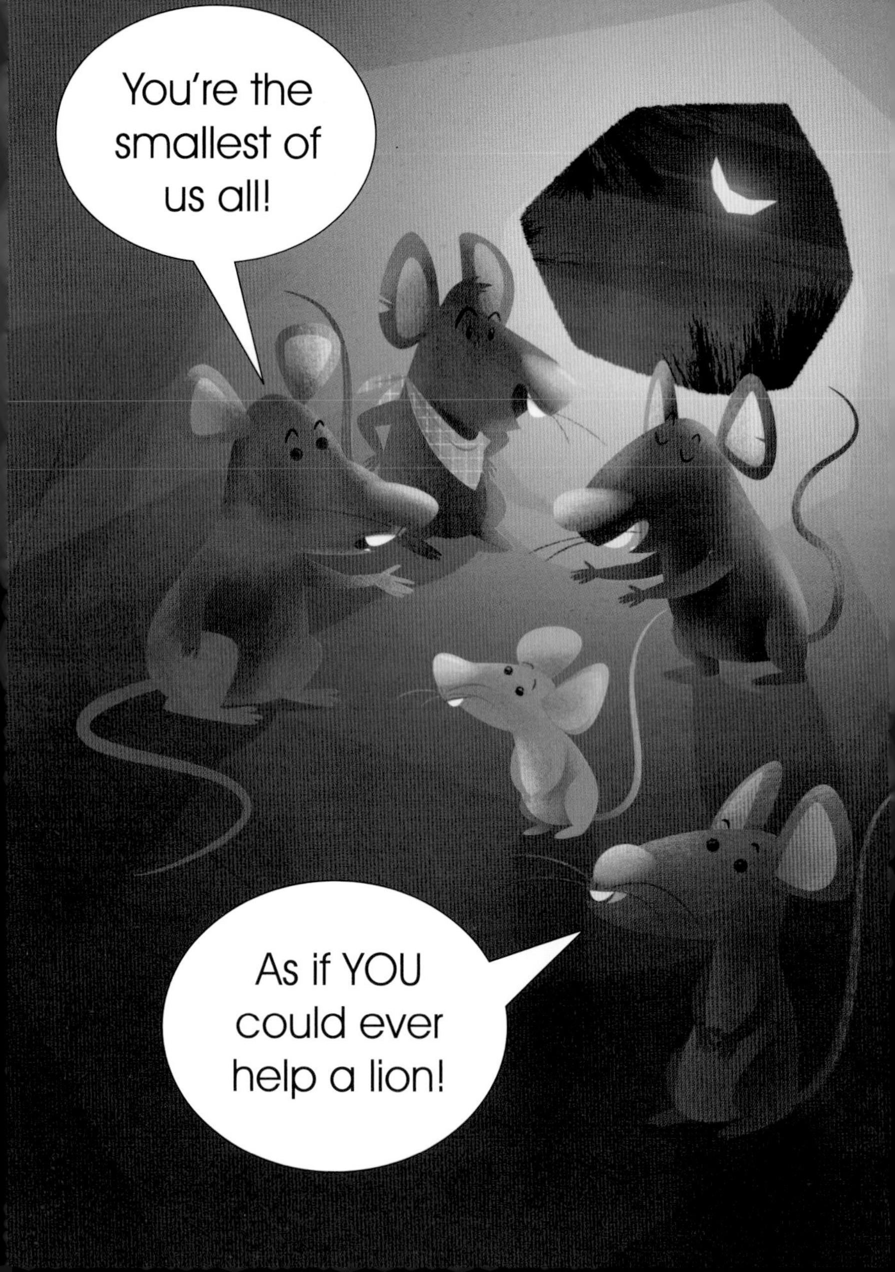

"Humph," said Little Mouse. "Just you wait and see."

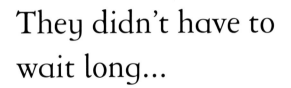

They didn't have to wait long...

That very night, Lion
walked straight into
a hunter's trap.

He thrashed and roared
and tried to claw his
way out.

The net held tight.

In his snug burrow, Little Mouse heard Lion's roars.

Roarrrrrrrrr!

"Lion is in trouble!" said Little Mouse. "I must go to him."

"You won't be able to help him," said Chief Mouse. "You're TOO SMALL."

"But I made a promise,"
said Little Mouse.

"And mice keep their
promises."

Little Mouse went
out into the night.

He followed the sound of
the roars.

At last, he found Lion
in a huge net.

"Have you come to laugh
at me?" snarled Lion.

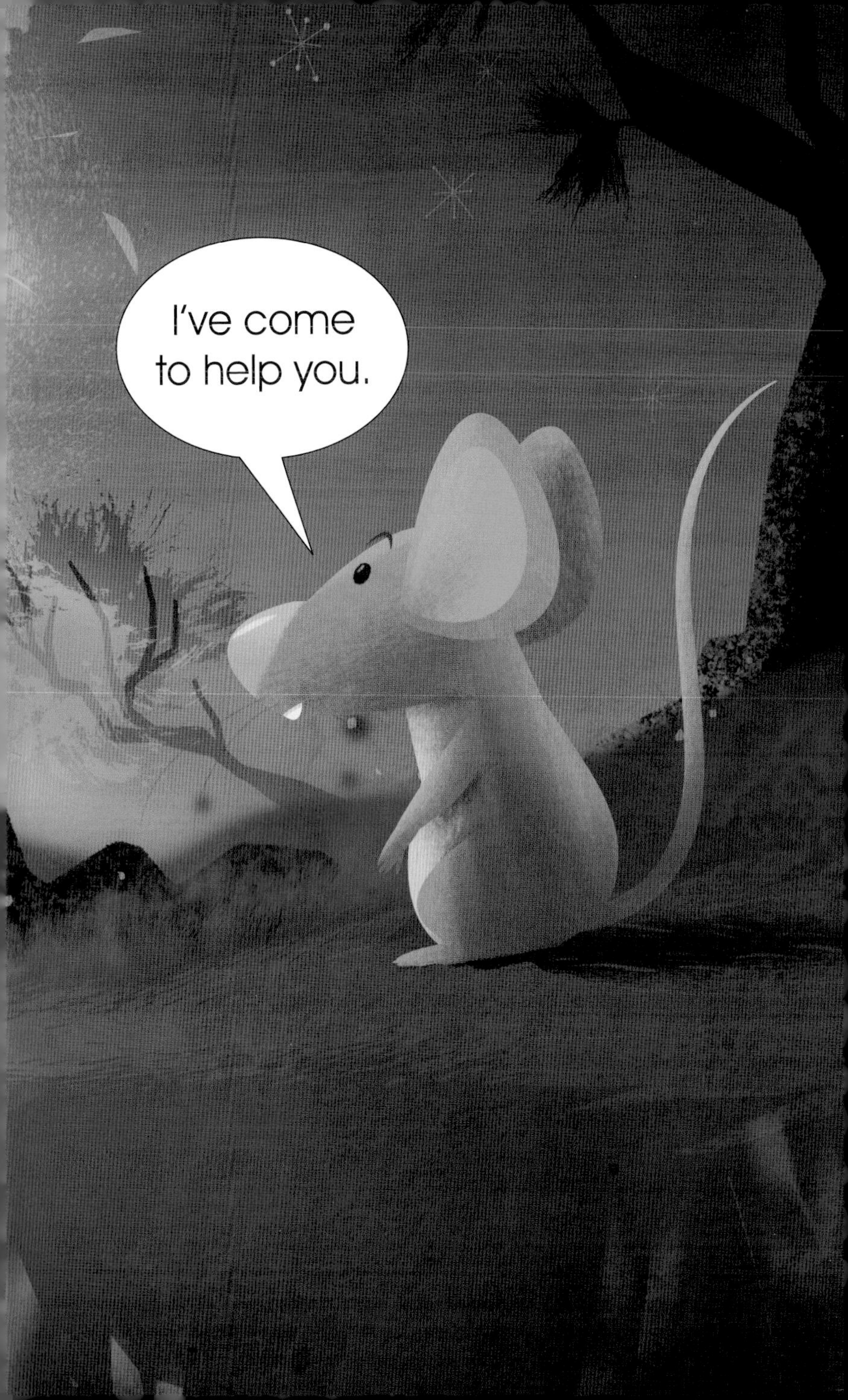
I've come to help you.

"No one can help me..." said Lion, sadly.

All night, Little Mouse
nibbled and gnawed at
the ropes.

At first light,
the net broke.

"You saved my life,"
said Lion.

42

"I see that little friends
can be great friends,
after all."

Little Mouse puffed
himself up with pride.

"Is there anything I
can do for *you*, Little
Mouse?" asked Lion.

"Actually," said Little Mouse. "There is *one* thing..."

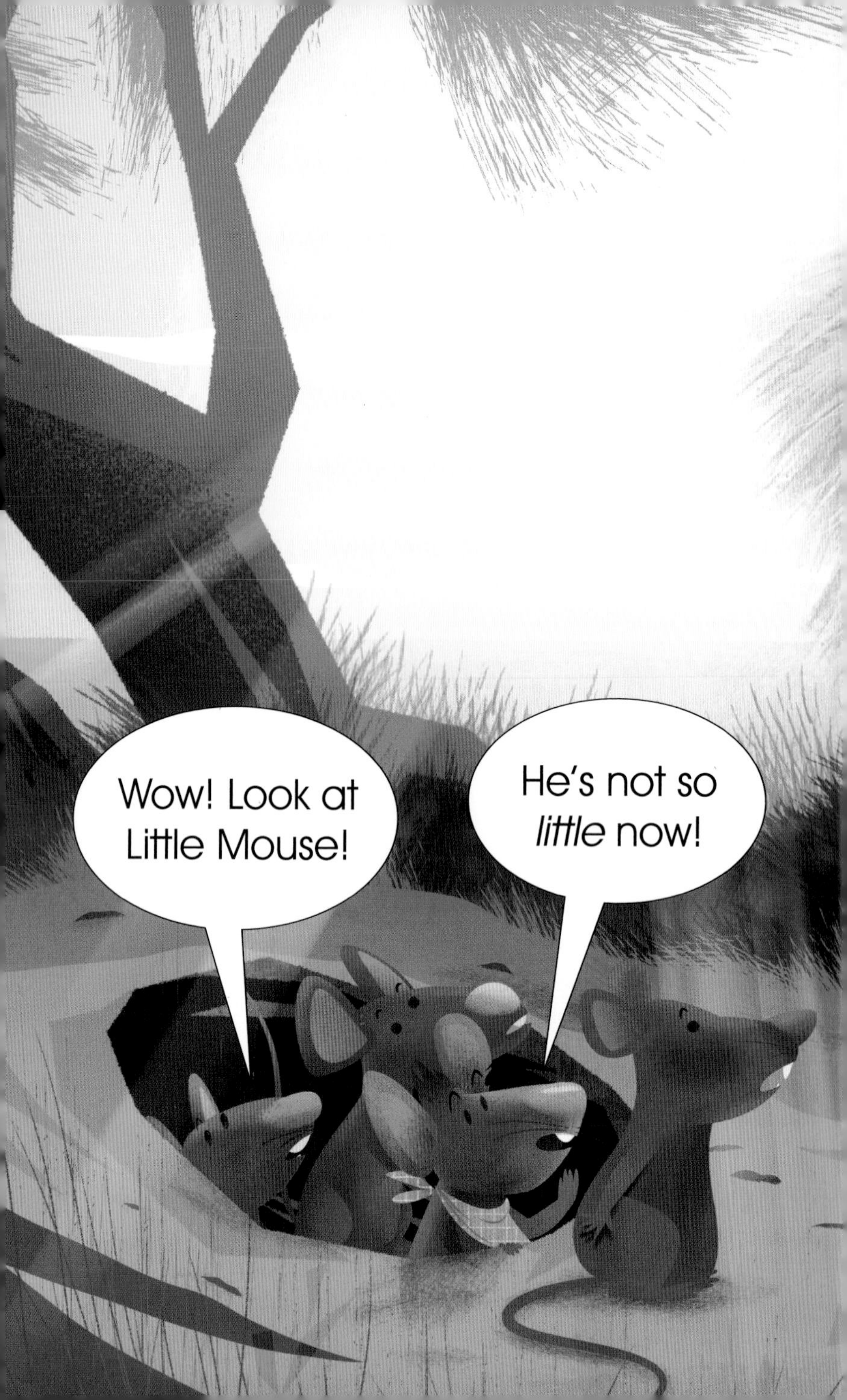
Wow! Look at Little Mouse!
He's not so *little* now!

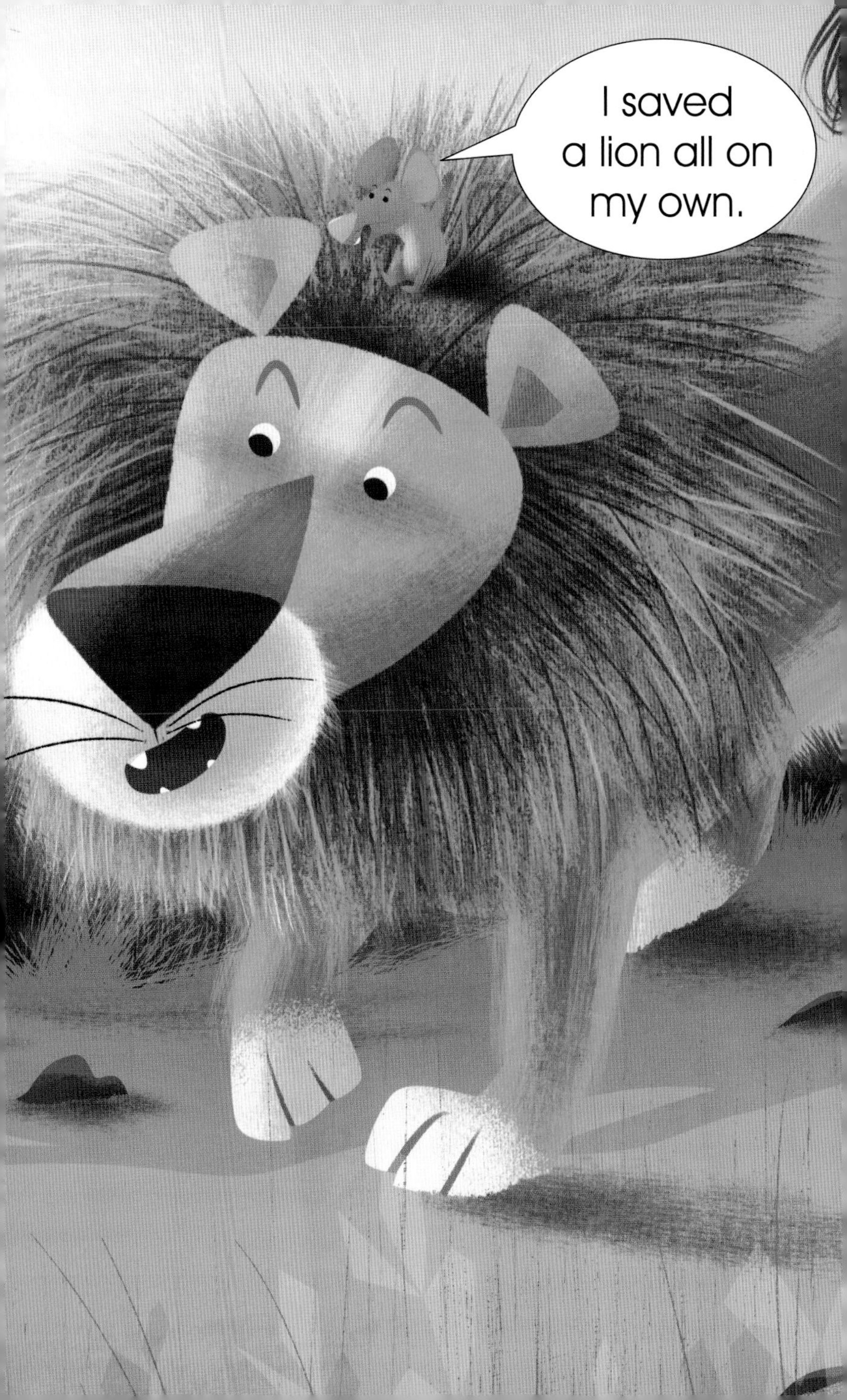
I saved a lion all on my own.

About the story

Aesop's Fables are from Ancient Greece. They always have a moral, or a lesson, at the end. The moral of this story is: "The small can help the strong."

Designed by Vickie Robinson
Series designer: Russell Punter
Series editor: Lesley Sims

First published in 2019 by Usborne Publishing Ltd., Usborne House, 83-85 Saffron Hill, London EC1N 8RT, England. www.usborne.com Copyright © 2019 Usborne Publishing Ltd.

USBORNE FIRST READING
Level Four